What Happened to Patrick's Dinosaurs?

What Happened

to Patrick's Dinosaurs?

by Carol Carrick
Pictures by Donald Carrick

CLARION BOOKS/ NEW YORK

To Eric and Kara

Clarion Books
a Houghton Mifflin Company imprint
215 Park Avenue South, New York, NY 10003

Text copyright © 1986 by Carol Carrick
Illustrations copyright © 1986 by Donald Carrick

For information about permission
to reproduce selections from this book,write to Permissions,
Houghton Mifflin Company, 215 Park Avenue South, New York, NY 10003.

Printed in the USA.

Library of Congress Cataloging-in-Publication Data

Carrick, Carol.
What happened to Patrick's dinosaurs?
Summary: Fascinated with dinosaurs, Patrick invents
an imaginary explanation of why they became extinct.
[1. Dinosaurs—Fiction] I. Carrick, Donald, ill.
II. Title
PZ7.C2344Wj   1986   [E]   85-13989
ISBN 0-89919-406-0   PA ISBN 0-89919-797-3

BVG 30 29 28 27 26 25

Patrick was helping his big brother, Hank, rake leaves.

"Where did they go?" asked Patrick.

"Who?" asked Hank.

"Dinosaurs, of course." Patrick never talked about anything else.

"Well, some people think the world got too hot for dinosaurs," said Hank. "And some think it got too cold. Maybe an asteroid hit the earth and covered it with dust." He showered Patrick with a pile of leaves.

"That's not what *I* think," said Patrick.

"And what do you think?" asked his brother.

"I think that, once upon a time, dinosaurs and people were friends," said Patrick.

"There weren't any people then," said Hank. "Cave men came much later."

"The people didn't live in caves," said Patrick. "Dinosaurs built them cozy houses."

"I suppose there were dinosaur houses, too," said Hank.

"That's silly," said Patrick. "Dinosaurs didn't live in houses. They just made them."

Hank smiled. "What happened when the dinosaurs got hungry?" he asked.

"They knocked down trees and planted bananas," said Patrick. "And they always shared. Can I have a bite?"

"Then dinosaurs invented cars," said Patrick, "because people couldn't run as fast as they could."

"Dinosaurs made cars?" said Hank. "Why not airplanes?"

"They did make airplanes," said Patrick.

"And they made roads for people to drive on."

"Dinosaurs were big and strong so they did all the work."

"If they did everything, what were the people doing all this time?" asked Hank.

"Oh, they got very bored," said Patrick. "So dinosaurs put on shows to make them happy. Some of the smart people learned to do tricks."

"Dinosaurs taught *people* tricks?"

WALTZING TRICERATOPS

"Dinosaurs wanted to teach people how everything works," explained Patrick. "But people were only interested in recess and lunch."

Hank lay down on a pile of leaves. Patrick lay down, too.

"Guess what happened then," Patrick said.

"I give up."

"Dinosaurs got tired of doing all the work," said Patrick. "And nobody would help them. So they built a big spaceship and left."

"Dinosaurs couldn't fit in a spaceship," said Hank.

"Then how could they leave?" asked Patrick.

"I didn't say they left," Hank said.

"But they did," said Patrick. "And they never came back."

"After a while people forgot that there ever were dinosaurs. They had to take care of themselves now, and they didn't know how."

It grew dark and the first stars came out. Hank and
Patrick watched as one bright star moved across the sky.
"You really think dinosaurs are out there?" asked Hank.
Patrick nodded. "But they miss us," he said. "And every
so often they check to see how we're doing."